Budge TROLL, Budge!

Level 5D

Written by Louise Goodman
Illustrated by Nicola Anderson
Reading Consultant: Betty Franchi

About Phonics

Spoken English uses more than 40 speech sounds. Each sound is called a *phoneme*. Some phonemes relate to a single letter (d-o-g) and others to combinations of letters (sh-ar-p). When a phoneme is written down, it is called a *grapheme*. Teaching these sounds, matching them to their written form, and sounding out words for reading is the basis of phonics.

Early phonics instruction gives children the tools to sound out, blend, and say the words without having to rely on memory or guesswork. This instruction gives children the confidence and ability to read unfamiliar words, helping them progress toward independent reading.

About the Consultant

Betty Franchi is an American educator with a Bachelor's Degree in Elementary and Middle Education as well as a Master's Degree in Special Education. Betty holds a National Boards for Professional Teaching Standards certification. Throughout her 24 years as a teacher, she has studied and developed an expertise in Phonetic Awareness and has implemented phonetic strategies, teaching many young children to read, including students with special needs.

Reading tips

This book focuses on the *j* sound (made with the letters *ge* and *dge*) as in bar**ge** and he**dge**.

Tricky and/or new words in this book

Any words in bold may have unusual spellings or are new and have not yet been introduced.

Tricky and/or new words in this book
would

Extra ways to have fun with this book

After the readers have finished the story, ask them questions about what they have just read.

Can you remember some words that contain the different sounds shown by the letter j?
Where did Gerald live?

Don't even think about eating me. I'm having a bad enough day already!

A Pronunciation Guide

This grid contains the sounds used in the stories in levels 4, 5, and 6 and a guide on how to say them.

/ă/ as in pat	/ā/ as in pay	/âr/ as in care	/ä/ as in father
/b/ as in bib	/ch/ as in church	/d/ as in deed/ milled	/ĕ/ as in pet
/ē/ as in bee	/f/ as in fife/ phase/ rough	/g/ as in gag	/h/ as in hat
/hw/ as in which	/ĭ/ as in pit	/ī/ as in pie/ by	/îr/ as in pier
/j/ as in judge	/k/ as in kick/ cat/ pique	/l/ as in lid/ needle (nēd'l)	/m/ as in mom
/n/ as in no/ sudden (sŭd'n)	/ng/ as in thing	/ŏ/ as in pot	/ō/ as in toe
/ô/ as in caught/ paw/ for/ horrid/ hoarse	/oi/ as in noise	/ʊ/ as in took	/ū/ as in cute

/ou/ as in out	/p/ as in pop	/r/ as in roar	/s/ as in sauce
/sh/ as in ship/ dish	/t/ as in tight/ stopped	/th/ as in thin	/th/ as in this
/ŭ/ as in cut	/ûr/ as in urge/ term/ firm/ word/ heard	/v/ as in valve	/w/ as in with
/y/ as in yes	/z/ as in zebra/ xylem	/zh/ as in vision/ pleasure/ garage/	/ə/ as in about/ item/ edible/ gallop/ circus
/ər/ as in butter			

Be careful not to add an /uh/ sound to /s/, /t/, /p/, /c/, /h/, /r/, /m/, /d/, /g/, /l/, /f/ and /b/. For example, say /fff/ not /fuh/ and /sss/ not /suh/.

Gerald the troll was large and orange. He lived under the bridge.

When anyone tried to cross
the bridge, he flew into a rage
and **would** not budge.

One day a badger on
a barge came to the bridge.
"Let me pass. I'm on a trip."

"Stop right there," said the troll.
"No badgers. I will not budge!"
Off he trudged.

A boy, jumping over
a hedge, came to the bridge.
"Let me pass. I'm late for lunch."

"Hold it!" said the troll.
"No hungry boys."
Off he trudged.

Next, a gingerbread man
came to the bridge.
"Let me pass. Have this fudge."

"Out!" said the troll.
"No gingerbread men."
Off he trudged.

A lady named Marge
slid to the bridge.
"Let me pass now," she said.

"Off with you!" said the troll.
"No ladies."
Off he trudged.

One day, a judge
came to the bridge.
"Let me pass. That's an order!"

"Back off," said the troll.
"I will not budge! Not even
for a judge." Off he trudged.

Someone else came to the bridge.

It was another troll.
He was orange. He was in a rage.
He was very, very large!

"Let me pass!" said the troll.

"Please do," said Gerald.

Off he trudged.

OVER 48 TITLES IN SIX LEVELS
Betty Franchi recommends...

Other titles to enjoy from Level 4

I love reading phonics — **The Maze** — 978 1 84898 771 5

I love reading phonics — **Fairy Fay's Bad Day** — 978 1 84898 772 2

I love reading phonics — **Eve the Knight** — 978 1 84898 773 9

Some titles from Level 5

I love reading phonics — **Snapped by Sam!** — 978 1 84898 775 3

I love reading phonics — **Max's Trip** — 978 1 84898 776 0

I love reading phonics — **George the Genius Gerbil** — 978 1 84898 777 7

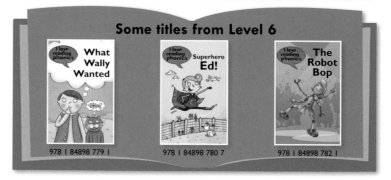

Some titles from Level 6

I love reading phonics — **What Wally Wanted** — 978 1 84898 779 1

I love reading phonics — **Superhero Ed!** — 978 1 84898 780 7

I love reading phonics — **The Robot Bop** — 978 1 84898 782 1

An Hachette Company
First Published in the United States by TickTock, an imprint of Octopus Publishing Group.
www.octopusbooksusa.com

Copyright © Octopus Publishing Group Ltd 2013

Distributed in the US by
Hachette Book Group USA
237 Park Avenue, New York NY 10017, USA

Distributed in Canada by
Canadian Manda Group
165 Dufferin Street, Toronto, Ontario, Canada M6K 3H6

ISBN 978 1 84898 778 4

Printed and bound in China
10 9 8 7 6 5 4 3 2 1